BOW WOW

A Day in the Life of Dogs

JUDY REINEN

Megan Tingley Books

 Little, Brown and Company
BOSTON NEW YORK LONDON

This book is dedicated to dogs everywhere,
who enrich our lives with their unconditional love.

And especially to Basil,
my faithful companion and best friend. You are such a delight.

First Edition

Library of Congress Cataloging-in-Publication Data
Reinen, Judy.
   Bow wow: a day in the life of dogs / Judy Reinen.
      p. cm.
   Summary: Photographs depict dogs in all sorts of human activities, from eating breakfast and getting dressed to going to the beach and watching television.
   ISBN 0-316-83290-1
   [1. Dogs — Fiction] I. Title.

PZ7.R27482 Do 2001   00-062438
[E]—dc21

10 9 8 7 6 5 4 3 2 1

TWP
PRINTED IN SINGAPORE

This book features full-color photographs of live dogs with sets designed and photographed by Judy Reinen. The breeds featured on each page are as follows: title page, West Highland white terrier; page 3 (l. to r.), shar-pei, Doberman, Tibetan terrier; page 4, English springer spaniel; page 5, American cocker spaniel; pages 6 and 7, rottweiler; pages 8 and 9, basset hound; page 10, bichon frise; page 11, Afghan hound; page 12 (l. to r. clockwise), bichon frise, chow chow, Tibetan terrier, Labrador retriever; page 13, Tibetan terrier and American cocker spaniel; page 14, English springer spaniel; pages 15, 16, and 17, golden retriever puppies; page 18, dalmatian; page 19, Samoyeds; page 20, Old English sheepdog; page 21, dachshunds; pages 22 and 23, shar-peis; pages 24 and 25, boxer; pages 26 and 27, Old English sheepdog; page 28, bearded collie; page 29, rough-coated collies; page 30, beagles; page 31, Chihuahuas; page 32, West Highland white terrier.

A big thank-you to the owners of all the dogs I have had the privilege of capturing on film. Your enthusiasm and support are greatly appreciated.
—J. R.

Have you ever wondered what dogs do all day? You probably think we just eat and sleep. Actually, a dog's day is just like yours! We took these pictures to show you....

We wake up early in the morning...

and wait for our breakfast to be served.

We always make our beds.

And help clean the house.

We take a long walk...

and then
have a little
snack.

We get our hair done.

Some of us like it curly.

Others like it long and straight!

We get dressed.

(It takes a while to find the right outfit.)

We help out in the garden.

We visit with the neighbors and...

invite them over
for parties!

We take care of our families.

And go
for a drive.

On nice days, we go to the beach.

We like to take a lot of naps.

By ourselves...

or with our friends!

At the end of the day, we always help make dinner.

After dinner,

we take a bubble bath.

We put on our pj's.

And watch our favorite shows.

Then it's bedtime.
Some of us sleep outside.

But we would rather be inside.
In *your* bed.